GRANDAD'S ISLAND

For Grandad

First U.S. edition 2016

Library of Congress Catalog Card Number pending
ISBN 978-0-7636-9005-2

16 17 18 19 20 21 TLF 10 9 8 7 6 5 4 3 2 1

Printed in Dongguan, Guangdong, China

This book was typeset in Adobe Caslon Pro.
The illustrations were created digitally.

Candlewick Press
99 Dover Street
Somerville, Massachusetts 02144

visit us at www.candlewick.com

GRANDAD'S ISLAND

Benji Davies

CANDLEWICK PRESS

At the bottom of Syd's backyard, through the
gate and past the tree, was Grandad's house.

There was a key under a flowerpot, and Syd could let himself in anytime he liked.

One day Syd stopped by
to see Grandad.

But he wasn't in any
of the usual places.

Then, just as he was about to
leave, Syd heard Grandad calling.

"Ah, there you are!" said Grandad.
"There's something I want you to see."

Syd carefully climbed up the ladder.
He had never been in Grandad's
attic before.

It was full of old boxes and things that
Grandad had collected from around the world.

At the far end of the attic, Grandad pulled a sheet
down from the wall to reveal a big metal door.
"After you, Syd," he said.

Syd turned the handle — *CLUNK* —
and gave the heavy door a push.

Syd found himself standing on the deck
of a very tall ship. There was an ocean of
rooftops all around.

Grandad pulled a handle.
BOOOOOOOOP! went the horn,
and the ship lurched forward.
"Steady as she goes!" Grandad boomed.

Grandad was very good at steering the ship and kept them on a smooth course across the rolling waves.

Mile after mile, all they saw was sea and sky, sky and sea—until, at last, something appeared on the horizon.

"LAND AHOY!"
shouted Syd.

They dropped the ship's anchor and
made their way to the shore.
"Grandad, don't you want your stick?" Syd asked.
"No, I think I'll be all right," said Grandad.

In the thick jungle of the island,
it was very hot.
"We must find a good spot for
a shelter," said Grandad.

At the top of the island, where a cool breeze
blew through the trees, they found an old shack.

There was a lot to do, but with a little help,
they soon had the place shipshape.

They explored the island
high and low. At every turn
they saw new wonders.

It was the most perfect place.
Syd wished they could stay forever.

But he knew that it would soon be time for them to leave.
"Syd, there's something I've been meaning to tell you,"
said Grandad. "You see . . .

I'm thinking of staying."
"Oh," said Syd. "But won't you be lonely?"

"No . . . no, I don't think I will,"
said Grandad, smiling.

Syd hugged Grandad one last time.
He would miss him very much.

When Syd set sail, everyone came to wave good-bye.

Across the waves, the ship chugged and churned.

The journey seemed much longer without Grandad.
But Syd steered the ship safely home.

The next morning, Syd went back over
to Grandad's house.

It was just the same as it had always been.
Except Grandad wasn't there anymore.

In the attic it was very quiet.
The big metal door wasn't there—
it was as if it had never been there at all.

Then Syd heard something tapping at
the window. He wondered what it might be.

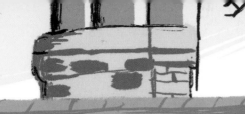

There, on the window ledge,
was an envelope.

Syd carefully pulled it open.